Dante Alighieri

Dante's Garden

with legends of the flowers

Dante Alighieri

Dante's Garden
with legends of the flowers

ISBN/EAN: 9783337080129

Printed in Europe, USA, Canada, Australia, Japan

Cover: Foto ©Andreas Hilbeck / pixelio.de

More available books at **www.hansebooks.com**

DANTE'S GARDEN

"DIPINSE GIOTTO IN FIGURA DI DANTE"

DANTE'S GARDEN

WITH

LEGENDS OF THE FLOWERS

BY

ROSEMARY A. COTES

" Let thy upsoaring vision range at large
This garden through: for so by ray divine
Kindled, thy ken a higher flight shall mount."

CARY.

" Vola con gli occhi per questo giardino:
Chè veder lui t'acconcerà lo sguardo
Più al montar per lo raggio divino."

Par. xxxi. 97.

METHUEN & CO.
36 ESSEX STREET, W.C.
LONDON
1898

TO

MY MOTHER

THIS LITTLE BOOK IS DEDICATED

WITH LOVE

THE English translations of the *Divina Commedia* used in this little collection of flower-legends are taken from Cary's *Vision of Dante*.

The author also wishes to express her indebtedness to Mr. Richard Folkard's book on *Plant Lore, Legend and Lyric*, from which she has derived much valuable help, and her gratitude to Mr. Paget Toynbee for kindly consenting to contribute a prefatory note.

The frontispiece is due to the courtesy of Messrs. Alinari of Florence, by whose kind permission their photograph of Giotto's portrait of Dante has been reproduced.

PREFATORY NOTE

IN this little volume a collection has been made of some of the passages in the *Divina Commedia* which give evidence of Dante's love for flowers, and trees, and all the details of plant-life. Dante was a close observer of Nature, and many of the most beautiful similes in his poem are drawn from his observations of the familiar phenomena of the garden and of the countryside. Even the gloom of his *Hell* is relieved by such pictures as those of the drooping flowers revived after a frost by the warmth of the sun (ii. 127–9),—the slowly falling leaves and "bare ruined choirs" of autumn (iii. 112–14),—the gale crashing through the woods and rending the branches (ix. 67–70),—the pastures covered with the thick hoar-frost (xxiv. 1–9),—the tenacious grasp of the ivy on the tree-trunk (xxv. 58–9),— while the descriptions in the *Purgatory* of the Terrestrial Paradise, with its wealth of flowers, and foliage, and grassy river-banks, are not surpassed for brilliancy of colouring even by the gorgeous flower-gardens with which we are familiar in the frescoes of Fra Angelico and of Benozzo Gozzoli.

7

PREFATORY NOTE

A special interest is added to the passages selected by the inclusion of the legends and traditions connected with the various flowers and plants mentioned by Dante. It is doubtful, however, to what extent Dante was himself acquainted with these. There is little trace in his writings of any knowledge on his part of plant-lore[1] (except, of course, such as is to be derived from classical sources, as in the case of the mulberry, for instance), though he was familiar enough with the kindred lore of the "bestiaries," as is evident from his references to the phœnix and the pelican. Sometimes, perhaps, a point has been stretched in order to include such flowers as the narcissus, the veronica, and the passion flower, to which Dante does not actually refer, but the reader will probably not be inclined to cavil on this account.

Those who know Dante only as the Poet of Hell will, we think, be grateful to Miss Cotes for her presentation of him here as the Poet of Flowers, a title not inappropriate to one whose native place was Fiorenza, the Flower-City.

PAGET TOYNBEE.

[1] A possible exception is his mention of the heliotrope in the Letter to the Princes and Peoples of Italy; but the reference in this case is probably not, as many think, to the flower, but to the gem, of that name.

CONTENTS

9

CONTENTS

DANTE'S GARDEN

" Let thy upsoaring vision range at large
This garden through . . ."

Par. xxxi. 97.

NO reader of the *Divina Commedia* can fail
to notice Dante's love for all the green,
fresh, scented things of the earth, and more
especially for flowers.

Throughout the latter part of the poem we
find him continually employing flowers, in three
distinct ways. First, for their colour—he con-
stantly uses them as examples of the delicate
tints he wishes to convey to the mind of the
reader. Then, for their emblematical significance—as he was accustomed to think of them
in association with the legends of the saints in
mediæval Church history, or as adorning heathen
mythology. And lastly, for the flowers them-

11

selves; for the love he bore them because they
were flowers, and because they were associated
in his mind with early aspirations of innocence
and purity.

Much in his writings leads us to imagine that
at some period of Dante's life there may have
been a garden that he knew and loved—a garden
to which his thoughts recurred with all the vivid-
ness of boyish impression, when, as a banished
man, and an outcast from home and country, he
wrote of early dawn, the scented earth, the leaves
all bending in one direction as the breeze passed
over them, and the song of the birds in the
trees.

Whenever he alludes to a garden, it is always
as a place of joy and innocence, a restful oasis
in his journey from the Inferno, and eventually
realised amongst his highest conceptions of
heavenly felicity.

Dante, speaking in the person of Adam, says
of the Terrestrial Paradise—

> " . . . Dio mi pose
> Nell' eccelso giardino, ove costei
> A così lunga scala ti dispose." [1]

" God placed me in that high garden, from whose bounds
She led thee up the ladder, steep and long."

---

[1] *Par.* xxvi. 109.

And in the same canto—

> " As for the leaves that in the garden bloom
> My love for them is great, as is the good
> Dealt by the eternal hand that tends them all."

> " Le fronde onde s'infronda tutto l'orto
> Dell' Ortolano eterno, am'io cotanto,
> Quanto da lui a lor di bene è pôrto." [1]

And again, speaking of St. Dominic, he calls him—

> " The labourer whom Christ in His own garden
> Chose to be His help-mate."

> " . . . Ed io ne parlo
> Sì come dell' agricola, che Cristo
> Elesse all' orto suo, per aiutarlo." [2]

Sometimes it is the garden of the Terrestrial Paradise, sometimes the garden of the Church, and sometimes that most exquisite and glorious garden of heaven itself—

> " . . . that beautiful garden
> Blossoming beneath the rays of Christ."

> " . . . il bel giardino
> Che sotto i raggi di Cristo s'infiora," [3]

the garden of which Dante says, " Heaven's decree forecasts" that it shall be filled eventually with all the spirits of the blest.

[1] *Par.* xxvi. 64.　　[2] *Par.* xii. 70.　　[3] *Par.* xxiii. 71.

DANTE'S GARDEN

There is a passage in the *Vita Nuova* in which Dante, after speaking of his first meeting with Beatrice, in his ninth year, says that he went many times in his boyhood to seek this most youthful angel, at the bidding of Love, who had then taken rule in his heart. May not these first meetings have taken place in a garden?—in the garden of Beatrice's Florentine home?

We have ample evidence in his writings that a garden existed somewhere in Dante's fancy, and that thither the poet would often retire in imagination, and wander along its paths, and refresh his weary soul with the springing green shoots, the leaves and herbs and flowers, which are brought so vividly before us in the *Purgatorio* and *Paradiso*.

Who would not have loved to roam with him here? What a store of legend and poesy and fancy must have hung around the plants and flowers of many lands in this garden of his, flowers whose seeds had been brought by the circling breezes from the Terrestrial Paradise.

The thought of a flower may be suggestive, as the pages of a missal in some ancient shaded library, whereon glow wondrous quaint illuminations, and brilliant, richly-coloured borders, with legends and old-world stories written between. For every flower has its history, which differs for each human soul that reads between the leaves.

Dante does not mention many flowers by name, nor any, without clear indication that he has dreamt and thought much over its legendary association, that to him it is not only a flower, but also the emblem of certain virtues or saintly qualities, or the graceful memento of some classical legend. In everything connected with Dante's flowers we have the mystic soul of the poet impressed upon us—the poet who sees more than the flower whilst gazing at the flower, and to whom the vision of its beauty opens avenues of thought, in which the object itself at times is swept away by the flood of fancy it produces.

In this manner we may interpret his allusions to the narcissus, the syringa, the veronica, and many others, where the poetical references are to the legends rather than to the flowers associated with the legends, yet one may suppose that the poet at the same time had in mind the dainty scented blossom, the green rush by the riverside, or the wild bird's-eye imprinted with the face of the Saviour, that ever turns its transparent petals towards the sky, and that he indulged the double fancy with a full appreciation of the additional beauty suggested, by the association of the legend with the flower.

DANTE'S GARDEN

The old well-known legends of the flowers, whether mythological or ecclesiastical, may well carry us back into Dante's garden, whither the poet, outcast and banished, would retire from the harsh realities of his daily life, and would wander in fancy at early dawn, when the leaves were full of the movement and song of the awakening birds, and whence, amidst the wealth of bloom and colour, he would select here a leaf and there a flower for the embellishment of his immortal poem.

THE ROSE

" No braid of lilies on their temples wreathed.
    Rather, with roses, and each vermeil flower,
    A sight, but little distant, might have sworn
    That they were all on fire above their brows."

            ". . . di gigli
    D'intorno al capo, non facevan brolo,
    Anzi di rose e d'altri fior vermigli:
    Giurato avria poco lontano aspetto,
    Che tutti ardesser di sopra da i cigli."
                            Purg. xxix. 146.

IT was the dream of the poet Anacreon, that
    Aurora dipped her finger-tips into the calyx
of the rose to colour them, and as translated by
St. Victor—

        " Des plus tendres de ses feux
            Venus entière se colore,"

Anacreon goes on to tell us how the earth first
came to produce this beautiful creation.

The wave having given birth to its glorious

B   17

goddess Cypris, and Minerva having sprung from the brain of Jupiter, Cybele could only oppose to the beauty of these two goddesses a tiny bud appearing upon a young shoot. But at the first sight of the nascent rose-bud Olympus smiled, and shed upon it nectar for dew. The young bud, thus watered from heaven, slowly opened, and upon its shining stem appeared the first rose, the queen of flowers, unfolding her petals in the summer sunshine.

To Dante the first flower in his garden is the rose, and this not for any mythological association, but because it represented to him the centre of his religion and faith. To him it is a flower full of mystery, the flower which Solomon sang, the rose blossoming in the garden of Paradise.

It represents in all his symbolism the Blessed Virgin.

> ". . . that fair flower, whom duly I invoke
> Both morn and eve . . . "

> ". . . quel bel fior, ch'io sempre invoco
> E mane e sera . . . "[1]

and to whom his Beatrice herself is but hand-maiden. A great governing fact in Dante's life is his love for Beatrice, but the keynote of his

[1] *Par.* xxiii. 88.

existence is his love for God. He says that the knitting of his heart to God has from the sea of ill-love saved his bark.

He employs the rose to describe the whole army of the saints, moving in advancing and receding circles, like a white rose unfolding and closing its petals. The thrones of all the blessed

> ". . . in a circle spread so far
> That the circumference were too loose a zone
> To girdle in the sun,"[1]

he compares to a rose with its leaves extended wide. The holy multitude in heaven seem to him

> "In fashion as a snow-white rose."

> "In forma di candida rosa."[2]

In pictured representations of the Blessed Virgin the lily is frequently introduced, as a fit emblem of grace and purity; but with Dante the lily is not sufficient. No pale colour, or the purity of white only, can express in his glowing imagery the mystery of humanity carried into heaven, or, in the person of the mother of our Lord, drawing heaven down to itself.

[1] *Par.* xxx. 103.　　　[2] *Par.* xxxi. 1.

THE ROSE

To him the Blessed Virgin is the rose.

> "... the rose,
> Wherein the Word divine was made incarnate."

> "... la rosa, in che'l Verbo Divino
> Carne si fece."[1]

These burning words do not express the pallor of the lily, but the full, glorious, scented bosom of the rose. Beatrice, with her eyes full of gladness, points out to him the mystic rose, in the garden of Paradise, blossoming under the rays of God.

In the canto before that in which Beatrice first appears and speaks with Dante, he describes a glorious vision of a triumphal procession of the Christian Church. In this vision roses and lilies both figure as crowns on the brows of the saints, and their comparative significance in his mind is clearly indicated.

The lily is the type of purity, only reached in heaven; but the rose is still first. For the rose includes everything: light and vivid colour, and purity above all, but purity that has blossomed forth into the living flame of heavenly love. The last seven spirits in the procession, who wear the red roses, no longer need

> "The braid of lilies on their temples wreathed,"

---

[1] *Par.* xxiii. 73.

but, at a little distance, it might have seemed that

"They were all on fire above their brows,"[1]

enwreathed with red roses—on fire with heavenly zeal and love. This is but in the Earthly Paradise. Later on, when Dante reaches heaven, he says that he feels love and adoration "full blossomed" in his bosom "as a rose before the sun,"

> ". . . When the consummate flower
> Has spread to utmost amplitude!"

> "Come il Sol fa la rosa, quando aperta
> Tanto divien quant' ell' ha di possanza."[2]

---

[1] *Purg.* xxix. 150.   [2] *Par.* xxii. 56.

THE OLIVE

" . . . In white veil with olive wreathed
 A virgin in my view appeared, beneath
 Green mantle, robed in hue of living flame."

  " Sopra candido vel cinta d'oliva
   Donna m'apparve, sotto verde manto,
   Vestita di color di fiamma viva."
        Purg. xxx. 31.

 " As the multitude
  Flock round a herald sent with olive branch
  To hear what news he brings."

  " E come a messaggier che porta olivo
   Tragge la gente per udir novelle."
        Purg. ii. 70.

OLIVE is the sign of peace, and when Dante
encircles Beatrice's brow with olive it is a
sign that she comes as a messenger of peace from
God to him.

Most of the countries in Europe have retained

different versions of the ancient Hebrew and Greek traditions of the tree of Adam.

This tree arose from the grave of our first parent, and the three rods of which it was composed were the olive, the cedar, and the cypress. These three rods grew together, and the cross of Christ was afterwards made of the tree they produced.

Sir John Maundeville writes: " The table " aboven His heved that was a fote and a half " long, on whiche the tytle was written in Ebrew, " Grece, and Latyn, that was of Olyve ;" and in another place he quaintly explains it: " The " table of the tytle thei maden of Olyve ; for " Olyve betokeneth Pes. And the storye of Noe " witnesseth whan that Culver broughte the " braunche of Olyve, that betokened pes made " betwene God and man. And so trowed the " Jewes for to have pes whan Crist was ded; for " thei sayd that He made discord and strife " amonges them."

The table of the title being made of olive has always been considered in the Church as an emblem of peace and reconciliation between God and man, over the dying body of Christ; and in many parts of Italy there still survive favourable superstitions with regard to an olive branch. The young girls use them for divination, and the peasants believe that no witch or sorcerer will enter a house where an olive branch that has been blessed is suspended. In Venetia it is considered a safeguard against storm and lightning, and amongst the ancient songs of Provence one — called the Reaper's Grace — is yet retained in their harvest festivals of the present day, recording the story of the tree of Adam, and the olive of which the title-board was made.

In Grecian and Roman mythology the olive is dedicated to Minerva. Virgil calls her "Oleae Inventrix," the originator of the olive, on account of an old tradition that she disputed the worship of the Athenians with Neptune, and when the god of the sea opened a salt spring in the rock of the Acropolis to show his power, Minerva caused a beautiful olive tree to spring from the ground. The gods held a council, and awarded the palm to Minerva, who became the tutelary deity of the Athenians, and from that time their rulers sought to turn them from warlike and seafaring pursuits to the cultivation of the soil and arts of peace.

Perhaps Dante remembered when he crowned Beatrice with olive, that thus from the olive might be said to date the glorious works of Cimabue and Giotto, since art in Italy derived

THE OLIVE

its first inspiration from the earlier art and civilisation of Greece, for which Greece was indebted to the sacred olive branch.

An olive tree grew in the temple of Minerva. When any Athenian went to consult the Delphic oracle he carried a branch of olive in his hand; and in the laws of Solon special directions were given for the proper mode of planting and nurturing the sacred tree.

A legend handed down from the earliest times records that when Adam was very aged he attempted to root up a large bush, and having strained himself in the effort, and feeling his end approaching, he sent his son Seth to the angel that guarded the gates of the garden of Eden, to beg for a little of the oil of mercy from the tree of life.

The angel refused, but sent a message to Adam to tell him that in later days the precious oil would be sent to his descendants, when the Son of God should visit the earth.

He then gave Seth three small seeds to place in his father's mouth after death, and told him to bury Adam near Mount Tabor in the Valley of Hebron.

This was done, and in a short time three rods appeared above the ground—a cedar, a cypress, and an olive tree. These did not leave the mouth of Adam, nor was their existence known, till Moses received orders of God to cut a branch from them. This branch exhaled a perfume of the promised land, and with it Moses performed many miracles, healing the sick, drawing water from the rock, etc. It was on the exact spot of Adam's grave that God appeared to Moses out of a burning bush, supposed to have been one of these miraculous trees.

After Moses' death the three rods remained unheeded in the Valley of Hebron till the time of King David, who, warned in a dream, went and found them there. He also performed miracles with them—healing the leprous, palsied, and blind. In some stories the three rods are supposed to have united in one large tree, typical of the Holy Trinity.

King David placed the young cedar tree in the temple, where thirty years afterwards Solomon was about to use it with the cedars of Lebanon in the glorious restoration of the ancient buildings. Here the Queen of Sheba saw it, and prophesied: "Thrice blessed is this wood on which the sins of the world shall be expiated!" The Jews were indignant at the suggestion of a degrading death in connection with the Messiah, and cast it into the " Probatica Piscina," the Pool of Bethesda, where it remained till the

day of Christ's condemnation, when it was taken
out to make the cross. During the time that
it remained in the Pool of Bethesda an angel
visited it periodically, and the water had
miraculous powers of healing all diseases.

Sir John Maundeville tells us that the church
of St. Katherine—which stood in his day in the
vicinity of Mount Sinai—marks the spot where
God revealed Himself to Moses, and in it were
many lamps continually kept burning. The birds
kept these lamps supplied with oil, bringing
sprays of olives in their beaks, from which the
monks distilled the oil. " For thei have of Oyle
" of Olyves ynow bothe for to brenne in here
" lampes, and to ete also; and that plentie have
" thei, be a Myracle of God, for the Ravens and
" Crowes and the Choughes, and other Foules of
" the Countree, assemblen there every yeer ones,
" and fleen thider as in pilgrimage ; and everyche
" of hem bringethe a Braunch of the Bays or of
" Olyve in here bekes, instede of Offryng, and
" leven hem there, of the whiche the monks
" maken grete plentie of Oyle, and this is a gret
" Marvaylle."

The stories which so interested the pious and
credulous soul of Sir John Maundeville had early
taken deep root in Italy, and Dante, when he
places the olive in his garden of imagery, employs

it always in its ecclesiastical significance as an emblem of peace.

> ". . . As when the multitude
> Flock round a herald sent with olive branch
> To hear what news he brings . . ."

Later, in the same sense, he places the olive as a wreath on the head of Beatrice when she descends to him as a glorious apparition from heaven, clothed in the colours of faith, hope, and charity, and wearing the emblem of eternal peace as a coronet around her brow.

THE VERONICA OR SPEED-WELL

> ". . . Like a wight
> Who haply from Croatia wends to see
> Our Veronica, and the while 'tis shown
> Hangs over it with never-sated gaze—
> . . . So gazed I then adoring."

> "Quale è colui, che forse di Croazia,
> Viene a veder la Veronica nostra
> Che per l'antica fama non si sazia
> Ma dice nel pensier, fin che si mostra :
> Signor mio Gesù Cristo, Dio verace
> Or fu sì fatta la sembianza vostra?
> Tale era io . . ."

Par. xxxi. 103.

OUT in the meadows in many country places grows a little wild flower deserving a special mention in Dante's garden, for upon its delicate blue petals is impressed the face of our Blessed Lord—only a faint and imperfect sugges-

29

tion of the face, the two eyes enclosed in the M, recording the word OMO, in the human features —no actual portrait of the Saviour; and yet this little plant bears the name of Veronica, and is dedicated to the saint whose love and sympathy preserved to us for all ages the likeness of the face of Christ.

Dante says, in a passage in the *Paradiso*,—when he has just met St. Bernard, and is about to behold a glorious vision of the Blessed Virgin,— that, " Like to one who haply from Croatia wends to see our Veronica, and while 'tis shown hangs over it with never-sated gaze," so he stood lost in adoring contemplation in heaven.

This Veronica he mentions is not the flower, but the miraculous handkerchief, with the likeness of the Saviour's face impressed upon it, probably the one in Rome, which attracted vast numbers of pilgrims from distant parts, to come and gaze, for once in their lives, upon what they believed to be the true features of their Lord.

The legend of St. Veronica—the most truly womanly saint of the calendar—relates that when our Saviour was on His way to Calvary He sank beneath the weight of the cross, and Veronica came forward, brave and tender, ready to acknow- ledge her allegiance amidst all His foes, and wiped the sweat from His brow with her hand-kerchief.

The story does not record what insults may have been showered upon her by the rabble around for this little act of womanly tenderness, but we are told that a representation of the face of our Lord appeared upon the handkerchief, and that it was ever after treasured as a wondrous memento of His passion. The handkerchief is supposed to have healing qualities, and in this particular the little medicinal field-flower veronica shares its miraculous virtues.

Around every glorious deed in the world's history poetical fancy has wreathed flowers of fervent imagination. Strange, indeed, if such a life as that of Christ should have escaped, and such stories, though too little authenticated, retain some touch of the fervent love of the early Church.

The legend of St. Veronica is extended to the little speedwell flower, said to have grown at the Saviour's feet, and to have received some drops falling from the sacred forehead.

The flower is of a most delicate blue colour. The centre is white, and from it spring two slender, ball-tipped stamens. At a little distance the effect of eyes, nose, and mouth is faintly produced upon its petals. The devout religionist of the Middle Ages, fancying he discerned the very face of his Lord gazing at him from the tiny azure flower,—as it might have been in a vision, from the blue of heaven,—exclaimed, "It is indeed the Vera Icon! Our Veronica that has taken root!"

THE LAUREL

".... O power divine!
If thou to me of thine impart so much
That of that happy realm the shadow'd form
Traced in my thoughts I may set forth to view;
Thou shalt behold me of thy favoured tree
Come to the foot, and crown myself with leaves."

"O divina virtù, se mi ti presti
    Tanto, che l'ombra del beato regno
    Segnata nel mio capo io manifesti,
    Venir vedraimi al tuo diletto legno,
    E coronarmi allor di quelle foglie,
    Che la materia e tu mi farai degno."

Par. i. 22.

THE favoured tree of the gods is the laurel, the crown of the mighty conqueror and of the poet.

The laurel was consecrated by the Greeks and Romans to every kind of glory; philosophers, warriors, even emperors, considered it the highest

C

33

honour to obtain the laurel wreath, and Dante foretells, at the commencement of his *Paradiso*, that he also will obtain such a crown, if the " powers divine " whom he invokes will enable his genius to complete his high theme.

Delphos, on the shores of the river Peneus, is famous for its laurel trees. Dante speaks of a wreath of the laurel as the " Peneian foliage," [1] gathered to grace the triumph of a Cæsar or to deck the brows of a bard.

The beautiful nymph Daphne was changed into a laurel tree. She rejected the addresses of Apollo, in spite of the magic of his wondrous music and the eloquence of his entreaties; and when pursued by him, she fled to the banks of the river Peneus, and invoked the protection of her sire. Peneus entreated the gods, who changed her into a laurel, which became henceforth the favoured tree of heaven. As an emblem of virtue and the graces of the mind, it has always been preeminent, and was considered a suitable crown for beauty to place upon the brows of a conqueror, and a meet reward for those who held intellectual and mental pursuits in higher esteem than the indulgences of wealth or luxury.

When Apollo reached the river's bank, and saw nothing but a waving laurel tree where

[1] *Par.* i. 33.

the beautiful Daphne should have been, he is supposed to have broken into the following lament :—

> " Puisque du ciel la volonté jalouse
>   Ne permet pas que tu sois mon épouse,
> Sois mon arbre du moins ; que ton feuillage heureux
> Enlace mon carquois, mon arc, et mes cheveux ! " [1]

---

[1] Saint-Ange, *Métamorphoses d'Ovide.*

THE LILY

" . . . 'From full hands scatter ye
Unwithering lilies:' and so saying cast
Flowers overhead, and round them on all sides."

" Fior gittando di sopra e d'intorno
Manibus o date lilia plenis."

Purg. xxx. 20.

THE tall white garden lily is by many supposed to be dedicated to St. Joseph, and
on account of its purity and grace it is also
used in mystic representations of the Blessed
Virgin.

The lily is the emblem of purity, and in
Christian art is employed in pictures of the
Annunciation, the adoration of the Magi, and
the enthronement of the Holy Child.

It is called the Madonna lily, and seems
specially connected with associations of the
mother of our Lord. Yet the legend of the

lily does not relate to the Blessed Virgin. It is dedicated in all ancient story to St. Catherine, whose name (from. the Greek καθαρος) signifies pure, undefiled, and who, as the inspirer of wisdom and good counsel in time of need, may be said to be the patron saint of those sweet flowers

> " . . . the lilies, by whose odour known
> The way of life was followed."

> " . . . li gigli
> Al cui odor si prese'l buon cammino." [1]

In the vision of St. Catherine, angels come forth to meet her wearing chaplets of white lilies; and it was through this flower that St. Catherine's father—Costis—became converted to Christianity, when all the arguments of the saint had failed to turn him from the errors of heathenism. Until that time the lily had been a scentless flower, and its powerful perfume is said to date back only as far as the fourth century, when through a miracle wrought in a vision, Costis was turned into the right path.

Costis was the emperor of Alexandria, and half-brother to Constantine the Great. He was extremely devoted to his daughter, whose studies he superintended, and whose extraordinary abil-

[1] *Par.* xxiii. 74.

ities afforded him a source of constant pride and pleasure.

The one great grief of Catherine's early days lay in the fact that while her arguments, drawn from Plato, Aristotle, and the Gospels, had reduced her seven masters to footstools at her feet, no arguments were of any avail with her father, who continued to worship his false gods. She prayed much and earnestly for him ; and at length one night Costis had a vision, in which he saw his daughter, with a book in her hand, walking by his side, and arguing with him, as was her wont, from Plato. But as he refused to listen to her, he perceived that the pathway they were pursuing suddenly diverged, one part leading down a flowery vale, and the other up a steep and stony incline.

Catherine left his side and turned up the steep and stony path, where she quickly disappeared from view.

Costis stood hesitating between the two ways, unable to make up his mind which direction to follow, when he was attracted by a delicate and subtle perfume proceeding, as it seemed to him, from some distant field of white objects far up the stony path, and dimly illumined by a light proceeding from the summit of the hill. He turned up the steep incline, and soon found himself in a garden of white lilies, stretching far up to the portals of a golden gateway, seeming to his enchanted gaze the very entrance to Paradise. Sinking down bewildered and overcome with penitence in the midst of the miraculously scented lilies, Costis resolved to renounce from henceforth his heathen gods, and serve the only true Christ. As he lay thus, Catherine came forth from the gateway, and led him by the hand into the Golden City.

When he awoke from his vision, Costis determined to be baptized, and he soon drew a multitude of his people with him into the path of Christianity—in those days, indeed, a hard and thorny way, leading too often to the cross of martyrdom ere the Golden City could be reached.

The scentless lily became henceforth the sweetest among flowers, and was dedicated by common consent to the martyred virgin, St. Catherine.

Dante considers the rose and lily to be equally the flowers of Paradise.

Before the purity of the lily, as in the wondrous mystic presence of the rose, his genius fails and trembles. When he sees the vision of the glorious multitudes, with Beatrice in their midst, descending from heaven and scattering lilies around them,—"A hundred ministers and messengers of life eternal,"—his thoughts involuntarily recur to the words of the poet Virgil, and he quotes—

" Manibus o date lilia plenis,"

at this supreme moment paying the final tribute to his faithful friend and guide, who has just left him. From this time Beatrice alone is to guide him forward into the higher regions he is now approaching.

With Beatrice alone he will enter Paradise. Dante has as yet not been fully purged from his sins, nor does he hold himself yet worthy to gaze upon the pure face of the lily. Its vision is dimmed for him through tears into a flooded, expansive light, like a pearl of unapproachable perfection. The lily is only reached in deed and in truth when Beatrice at length descends to him, and then the glory of the mystic rose begins to blend with the purity of the lily.

The rose has not yet triumphed, but Dante is at peace, and his soul is satisfied.

Beatrice could show that in heaven may be reached the glistening heights where earthly love so seldom finds a foothold.

THE PLUM

" Thereat a little stretching forth my hand
   From a great wilding gather'd I a branch,
   And straight the trunk exclaimed: 'Why pluck'st
      thou me?'"

" Allor porsi la mano un poco avante
   E colsi un ramicel da un gran pruno,
   E il tronco suo gridò: 'Perchè mi schiante?'"

Inf. xiii. 31.

THE wild plum tree of the fields and hedges,
growing neglected and unpruned, is the
plant to which Dante so continually alludes as
a type of all that is rude and uncared-for.

In one instance, however, he speaks of it in
a more gracious and hopeful strain, when he says
he has seen it frowning all the winter long, yet
in the spring "bearing a blossom upon its top."[1]
The blossom of the plum appears before its leaf,

[1] *Par.* xiii. 135.

and upon the black and frowning twigs the tender white of an exquisite flower is a singularly beautiful suggestion of hope in circumstances however dark.

In Italy, where the plum is the commonest and wildest of trees, it is natural to think of it generally as an uncultured plant that grows outside the garden, in the same way that we regard the bramble—in spite of its blackberries beloved of children—as a type of ruin and neglect. Dante places the souls of those who have done violence to their own persons by committing suicide, in the Inferno, imprisoned in wild plum trees, where the Harpies build their nests, and torment the unfortunate trees by feeding on their leaves. The plucking of a leaf or bough causes the imprisoned soul intense pain, and one of the most pathetic scenes Dante records of his visit to the Inferno is where he by chance plucks a bough from one of these " wildings," and the trunk cries out and reproaches him with cruelty in thus causing it unnecessary torture.

Virgil apologises for his pupil, and in the subsequent conversation they hold with the tree (in which the soul of Piero delle Vigne is enclosed), the trunk informs them of the manner in which the luckless suicidal souls are cast down into the wood in the form of seeds, where they take root,

" with no place assigned them," and grow into these neglected trunks.

The plum has always been supposed to be an ill-omened tree, and the traditions of nearly all the European nations coincide on this point. In Germany it is thought unlucky to dream of plums, and in England there is an old rhyme which says—

> " Mony sloanes
> Mony groanes,"

meaning that ill-luck must be expected in a year in which wild plums are plentiful. The Italians generally despise this common fruit, and in Spain the sight of a wild plum tree growing across one's path is considered sufficient reason for postponing a journey to a later date, lest misfortune should overtake the traveller.

It is difficult to find a place for this plum of ill-omen in Dante's garden, unless it be as a type of the misfortunes that rendered so great a part of his life barren and unlovely. It must not infringe the fragrant borders where grow the roses and lilies of Paradise. But in the hedge outside, which encloses the " gold, fine silver, scarlet, and pearl white " [1] of the many flowers in his cultured borders, it may grow, and cast the shadow of its wild branches over the " fresh

[1] *Purg.* vii. 73.

emerald by herbage and flowers" planted where the poet delights to linger.[1]

In early spring, when he raises his eyes and sees a tender white blossom adorning the frowning wintry boughs before a leaf has ventured forth, the wild plum, with this little emblem of hope and courage upon it, will serve to remind him that no life is too hopeless for joy to blossom in it.

[1] *Purg.* vii. 75.

THE MARGUERITE OR DAISY

" . . . Amid those pearls
One, largest and most lustrous, onward drew."

" E la maggiore, e la più luculenta
Di quelle margherite innanzi fèssi."

Par. xxii. 28.

WHEN St. Augustine first came to England, all the woods were filled with singing-birds, and he loved to roam in them from his monastery in Canterbury, and watch the little brown birds engaged in their matin services, and listen to their happy notes, while he thanked God for the music and the singing and the sunshine.

One day, having wandered into a wood, he came unexpectedly out into the open, where the sun was shining brilliantly in contrast to the dark shadows of the trees he had left, and before him

45

lay spread a meadow filled with daisies in full bloom.

At the sight of these hundreds of little pale spheres, scattered over the meadow, the saint was suddenly overpowered, and, falling upon his knees, exclaimed, " Behold, a hundred pearls, with the radiance of a living sun in each ! So may the spirits of the blest shine in heaven ! "

Dante, in one of his visions in Paradise, sees St. Benedict, St. Francis, and others, appearing to him in

> " A hundred little spheres, that fairer grew
> By interchange of splendour . . . "[1]

and tells us, amidst these " Margherites," one " largest and most lustrous," the soul of St. Benedict, approached to speak to him. He also speaks of the heaven of Mercury, containing many spirits of the blest as a marguerite—

> " Within the pearl that now encloses us,
> Shines Romeo's light . . . "

> " E dentro alla presente Margherita
> Luce la luce di Romeo . . . "[2]

On his tours round the south of England, when St. Augustine entered a village, the children came forth to meet him crowned with wreaths of

[1] *Par.* xxii. 23.   [2] *Par.* vi. 127.

daisies; and on one occasion, when preaching in the open air to a large audience, he chose the daisy for his text, and beckoning to a small boy who carried a daisy-chain in his hand to come near, he held the chain up to the assembled multitude, and slowly drew the flowers, which were strung together by their stalks, one from the other.

"The sun," he said, "has imaged himself in the centre of each of these flowers, as the Sun of Righteousness will image Himself in each of your hearts. From this sun in the daisy white rays spread round. So may the rays of purity and goodness spread around you, reflected from the light of heaven within you. And as these flowers are strung together in a chain, so may you in England be united to each other, and to the holy churches of the world, by a chain that shall never be broken. And, unlike the feeble stems of these daisies that a child's fingers can sever, may the links of your chain be indissolubly connected, not to be broken, though strained and divided in the ages to come, until the great Creator of your being shall bring you all safe into His everlasting kingdom."

St. Augustine's Day is kept on May the 26th, in the bright spring-time, and all our associations connected with this saint, and the early days of

the revival of Christianity in England, lead us
to the beginning of the year and the fresh spring
flowers that rose from the chilly earth to welcome
him to our shores.

Dante also loves the spring. His thought of
heaven is of an ever-enduring springtide, and he
speaks of the flowers he saw in Paradise,

> " . . . that with still opening buds
> In this eternal springtide blossom fair,"

> " . . . che così germoglia
> In questa primavera sempiterna,"[1]

as a dream of perpetual renaissance.

In our calendars of the saints there are no less
than six St. Margarets ; and by popular tradition
the marguerite is supposed to be dedicated to one
of these. The saint whose special day is kept in
the blooming of the moon-daisies, July 20th, the
St. Margaret of the Dragon, was the daughter of
a heathen priest of Antioch. When she embraced
Christianity, her father drove her from his house,
and she retired to the cottage-home of her foster-
mother in the country, and there lived until
her martyrdom, doing simple duties — like the
simple daisy—with her face ever turned heaven-
ward.

The daisy of St. Margaret—the daisy conse-

[1] *Par.* xxviii. 115.

crated to innocence and childhood—Dante passes over; but to the marguerite which is a star—the daisy glorified, innocence restored after the dark wood of experience has been traversed—he recurs with ever-increasing joy.

THE IVY

" . . . Ivy ne'er clasped
A doddered oak, as round the other's limbs
The hideous monster intertwined his own."

" Ellera abbarbicata mai non fue
    Ad arbor sì, come l'orribil fiera
    Per l'altrui membra avviticchiò le sue."

Inferno, xxv. 58.

IVY—in Greek *Kissos*, the name of the infant
Bacchus—was dedicated to that god, and
used in bacchanalian revels equally with the vine.

Its property, however, was opposed to the
inebriating effects of intoxicating liquors, and in
the Middle Ages a concoction of ivy-berries taken
beforehand was supposed to prevent the possi-
bility of intoxication at a midnight carouse. The
ivy-bush outside taverns was placed there with
this idea ; and a favourite experiment was to
drink wine in an ivy cup, the ivy being thought
to have so great an antipathy to wine as to

separate it from the water, which immediately soaked through the cup, leaving only the wine behind.

There was a generally received opinion in the Middle Ages that ivy was a favourable plant of good omen ; it was used in the decoration of churches, and a mediæval carol runs thus—

> " Ivy is soft and meke of speech,
> Ageynst all bale she is blisse :
> Well is he that may hyre rech
> Veni Coronaberis !

> " Ivy berythe berries black :
> God grant us all His blisse—
> For there shall we nothing lack
> Veni Coronaberis ! "

Dante uses the ivy only as a simile of a clinging and tenacious plant, and if there was any special legendary association in his mind connected with it, it was probably only as applied to the bacchanalian feasts of the ancients. Still, the following little story in connection with his native city seems to find a suitable place here.

On the walls of an ancient convent some miles out of Florence the ivy had grown continually for centuries. A tradition had arisen that should the ivy cease to cling around a certain patriarchal tree in the monastic garden, the walls of the monastery would also be divested of their covering, and the whole place would fall to ruins.

It happened about the twelfth century that a terrible pestilence raged in the neighbourhood, but the rules of this special monastic order prohibited the brothers from relaxing their regular routine of discipline and study, even to render assistance to the sick and dying around them. Many acts of heroism were indeed performed by individual members of the community in their short hours of relaxation, but no regular system of attendance or hospital care was instituted.

The story relates that one day a plague-stricken family presented themselves at the gates of the monastery and demanded admittance. They were told that they might repair to the gardens, where food would presently be brought to them, and remain for shelter in one of the summer-houses or arbours if they wished, but that it was the hour for prayer, and no brother could be spared to attend to them at the moment.

The wretched family dragged themselves into the beautiful gardens, brilliant with summer flowers in full bloom; but no one appearing for a full hour to relieve them, they cursed the monastery and all its inmates, the flowers, the fountains, and the sunny lawns, since there were no beds where they could stretch their fevered limbs to die in peace, refreshed by the sacred offices of the Church. One of the men, who still had strength to wield an axe, cut the famous ivy stem, whose tradition was well known in the neighbourhood, through, to the bark of the tree it encircled, and then sank down on the ground at its foot, to await the arrival of the tardy brothers.

When at length, prayer being over, the monks arrived upon the scene, such assistance as they could render was immediately given to the uninvited guests; but the ravages of the pitiless plague had already reached a stage beyond human remedy, and before night death had relieved the unfortunate visitors one and all from their sufferings.

The following morning great was the consternation of the prior and all the inmates of the monastery to find the ancient ivy tree withering upon its stem and cut through to the root. A presentiment of coming misfortune seized the whole community, and the aged father, calling all the brothers of the order around him, said, "My sons, we have failed in our duty to man, whilst too eagerly aspiring to join with the angels in the worship of heaven. Did not our Blessed Lord Himself command us to render service to the least of these His brethren, saying that He would count it as rendered to Himself? From this time the hours of prayer will give place to the urgent necessity of nursing our plague-stricken neighbours, and may the blessing of God accompany our efforts."

From this time the brothers gave themselves up zealously to nursing and good works, and great assistance was rendered to the poor by the now devoted ministrants from the monastery. The plague ran its destructive course, and by degrees penetrated to the cells where the brothers knelt at night in prayer. One by one they succumbed to its virulent attacks, and at length not one remained alive of the former occupants of the ancient monastery. Decay invaded its precincts. The ivy on its walls withered, and at the present day picturesque ruins beautifully situated in still luxuriant gardens are all that remain to tell the tale of former splendour.

THE CROWN IMPERIAL

"Yellow lilies . . ."

"I gigli gialli . . ."

Par. vi. 100.

WHEN the drooping head of the tufted crown imperial is raised, five brightly shining drops of water may be seen within the cup of the flower, hanging like tear-drops around the centre.

The crown imperial grows stiffly and upright, and the curious tuft at the top suggests the fancy that at one time the flowers grew with their brilliant flame or sulphur coloured calyx turned upwards to greet the morning sunshine, instead of, as now, drooping around their stem.

When our Saviour was crucified, and darkness fell over the earth, all the flowers bowed their heads that they might not behold the terrible deed. Only the crown imperial remained up-

55

right, gazing proudly at the sky, until an angel came down, and, touching its haughty head with trembling fingers, dropped tears upon its flaunting petals.

From that time the crown imperial has ever bowed its head, overcome with remorse and sorrow, and the angel's tears are renewed continually in its drooping calyx.

All lilies that bow their graceful heads in every country are dear to Dante. He mentions them again and again in every variety, from the "yellow lilies" of the royal standard of France, to the white wild lilies of the meadow.

The crucifixion of Christ is also a subject very near to the heart of Dante. He says—

"Earth trembled at it, and the heaven was opened."

"Per lei tremò la terra, e'l ciel s'aperse."[1]

And he speaks often of the sufferings that our Lord underwent to gain that fair Bride, the Church, "Who with the lance and nails was won," "Che s'acquistò con la lancia, e co'chiavi,"[2] and of the "blest limbs that were nail'd upon the wood."[3] The lily of the crown imperial is the flower that carries us back in memory to the

[1] *Par.* vii. 48 (trans. Longfellow).
[2] *Par.* xxxii. 129.　　[3] *Par.* xix. 105.

darkness and suffering of the death of Christ, as its sister, the white lily of St. Catherine, raises our thoughts to the beauty and purity of the heaven that was opened to us through earthquake and pain.

In one of his outbursts of indignation at some of the errors of the Church, Dante makes Beatrice complain that legends were told in the Florentine pulpits more freely than the gospel was preached there.

> "One tells how at Christ's suffering the wan moon
> Bent back her steps, and shadowed o'er the sun
> With intervenient disk . . . "[1]

Yet in spite of his complaints of this, and other uncertainly authenticated tales, a curious glimpse is afforded us into the complex character of the man, when we find him using nearly the same symbolism himself in another canto, where he places the mystic eclipse in heaven, instead of on earth, and makes Beatrice and all the heavenly host lose splendour and light with sympathetic indignation at St. Peter's description of the corruption of the Church.

> "And such eclipse in heaven methinks was seen
> When the Most Holy suffered!"

> "E tale eclissi credo che in ciel fue,
> Quando patì la suprema Possanza!"[2]

---

[1] *Par.* xxix. 97. [2] *Par.* xxvii. 35.

THE RUSH

"Go therefore now, and with a slender reed
See that thou duly gird him, and his face
Lave, till all sordid stain thou wipe from thence."

"Va dunque, e fa che tu costui ricinghe
D'un giunco schietto, e che gli lavi'l viso,
Sì ch' ogni sucidume quindi stinghe."

Purg. i. 94.

THE flowering rush, known by the name of Acis, is the dwarf species of Amaryllid. The classical fable of the transformation of the young shepherd Acis into a river, on whose banks the flowering rush first appeared, was probably known to Dante. The sea-nymph Galatea was beloved by Acis, but the Cyclops, Polyphemus, also loved her, so hurled a broken piece of rock at Acis and slew him. From the rock that had crushed him a river issued forth, and from the blood of Acis arose the first flowering reed.

"The stone was cleft, and through the yawning chink
New reeds arose on the new river's brink."

Yet to Dante the rush, like nearly every flower or leaf he mentions, has a mystic and spiritual significance, and he uses it in the passage quoted above as an emblem of humility.

This plant seems to have a peculiar significance, since it is the first green object, cool and fresh, emerging from the lucid water, that greets Dante's eyes when he steps forth from the dark abyss of the Inferno into the less gloomy regions of Purgatorio, whence he is to be led eventually to the beautiful garden of the Earthly Paradise, as a preparation for the greater glories of heaven.

The garden of the Earthly Paradise will be gay with flowers, but on his first entry into Purgatorio, where punishment is yet to be endured, no flowers or bright colours greet his eyes. The cool green rush, with which it is commanded that he shall be girt, and the sight of water —the distant trembling of the ocean—and the air of the upper world, cause him sufficient joy and relief.

He explains clearly the meaning of the rush in the passage where he tells us that no other plant but one of a humble and bending nature could stand the flow of the water, no plant

> ". . . hardened in its stalk
> There lives, not bending to the water's sway."

Dante has a particular feeling and appreciation for the beauties of a river's bank, and some of the passages where he describes a running stream are so full of close and graceful observation of nature as to lead to the idea that they may have been written on the shores of a stream, within sight of the little islet on whose oozy bank, where the wave beats it, stores of rushes grow, or possibly from some loving memory of his boyhood.

Later, when he reaches the Earthly Paradise, again his steps are

> " Bounded by a rill, which to the left
> With little rippling waters bent the grass
> That issued from its brink . . . "

This is the river Lethe, and he describes gazing across its banks to a level meadow filled with flowers on the opposite shore, as only one could describe it to whom the scene was a reality and no dream; the transparency of the water and the brown colour it takes from the shadow of the trees overhead are most true to nature. In Dante's garden a little river ever flows " bruna, bruna," beneath the dark shade of the overhanging foliage, and on its banks the varying tints of May make perpetual spring-tide.

THE RUSH

When heaven at length is reached, the shadows disappear, and here

> "... I looked,
> And in the likeness of a river, saw
> Light flowing, from whose amber-seeming waves
> Flashed up effulgence, as they glided on
> 'Twixt banks on either side painted with Spring
> Incredible how fair; and from the tide
> There ever and anon, outstarting, flew
> Sparkles instinct with life; and in the flowers
> Did set them, like to rubies chased in gold."

> "E vidi lume in forma di riviera
>   Fulvido di fulgore, intra due rive
>   Dipinte di mirabil primavera.
>   Di tal fiumana uscian faville vive,
>   E d'ogni parte si mettean ne' fiori,
>   Quasi rubini, ch' oro circonscrive."
>
> *Par.* xxx. 61.

THE VIOLET

" .   . A hue more faint than rose,
   And deeper than the violet . . . "

"Men che di rose, e più che di viole."

Purg. xxxii. 58.

" MORE faint than rose, and deeper than
the violet!" Dante is speaking in
this place of the colour that the tree of knowledge assumed, when it suddenly burst into
flower, in one of his visions in the Terrestrial
Paradise. The word "deeper" signifies less
ethereal, with more of the life-colour, rose or
red, blended with the blue. He describes the
glorious colour of the sky at sunrise, less than
roses, and more than violet; the rose-colour of
the apple-blossom, slowly growing against the
blue of the sky, upon a leafless tree; the colour
of the thickening shoots, pale mauve in spring,
when a faint blue mist rises, and half-conceals
the close, slender twigs at the top of the trees;

52

or the colour of the sunset, when pink floods the blue of the darkening heaven.

Dante gazes, enrapt, at this vision of colour, and, slowly, unearthly music possesses his senses. He hears a hymn of such rare harmony as never yet was sung by mortal voices. It seems to him to blend into the perfect colour. The violet notes of multitudinous vibration are too ethereal to be retained by mortal senses, and, unable to endure it to the end, he sinks into a deep slumber.

Though it is certain that Dante of the thirteenth century could not have known definitely the theory of colour and vibration, yet it is a curious instance of the prophetic instinct, nay, inspiration, of the true poet, which leads him to dream of music blended into the rich vibrating tints of violet light, and thus to agree with Mendelssohn, who in later years held that violet is the supreme colour of music.

Certain pulsations in the ether produce a faint appearance of colour, as the harmonies of music are produced by vibration, and if we could arrive at the highest and purest notes beyond the regions of human perception, where only dream-spirits could follow us, we should be landed in a heaven of colour, "men che di rose, e più che di viole."

THE VIOLET

Mendelssohn, the most poetical of musicians, adopting this idea, playfully called his highest-stringed instrument, "the Violet," pretending that with it he could scale the regions where sound and colour meet.

The violet is dedicated to Orpheus with his lute, and the legend also leads us into a realm of music. Dante only mentions Orpheus once in his *Divina Commedia*, and then it is to place him in Limbo as an unbaptized soul, in company with many other poets and heroes of old.

When Orpheus, with his lute, charmed all the birds and beasts, and woods and mountains, the flowers also arose, and danced in a magic circle round him. And when he sank down, wearied, upon a bank to sleep, upon the spot where his enchanted lute had fallen there sprang into bloom the first violet, which, though the embodiment of purest music, yet is for ever mute, and nestles down amidst its leaves, listening to the ever-lasting harmonies of Nature.

THE FIG TREE

" . . . For amongst ill-savoured crabs
It suits not the sweet fig tree lay her fruit."

" . . . Chè tra li lazzi sorbi
Si disconvien fruttare al dolce fico."

Inferno, xv. 65.

IN the context of the quotation given above,
Dante makes his master, Latini, speak
somewhat bitterly of the way his pupil's work
will probably be received by his contemporaries;
though he also makes him say—

" If thou follow but thy star,
Thou canst not miss at last a glorious haven."

Dante did indeed " follow his star," and reached
a fame which has not been dimmed by five
intervening centuries.

This is not his only mention of the fig tree, as
in a later canto of the *Inferno* he alludes to an

E 65

Italian proverb, "A date for a fig," meaning that every man will receive a due reward of his works.

The fig tree, sweet and nourishing for food, has many associations in biblical parable and ancient story. In the East it is an emblem of home and plenty. Like the vine upon the walls of a man's house, the fig tree in his garden suggests prolific harvests and general prosperity, and the withering of a fig tree has always been supposed to be a sign of a coming blight in a man's fortunes.

A late traveller in Afghanistan, on his return to India, happened to encounter an Afghan chief, whom he had known in his travels in the North.

In order to remind the Afghan of their former intercourse, he asked of his well-being, and reminded him of the little house "under the fig tree" where he had so kindly entertained him some years before.

The chief's face fell, and in the simple phrase, "the fig tree is withered," informed his friend of his loss of fortune, and how, since their meeting, his home had broken up and his family had been scattered.

In Italy, too, the fig tree is regarded as an emblem of prosperity; and in the use Dante makes of it, saying that it ill-suits the sweet fig tree to lay her fruit among wild crabs, there is a pathetic allusion to his loss of home and the writing of his great work on alien soil.

The fig tree has been known to live to an extraordinary age. There are many fig trees famous for their life of centuries, and the fruit is not supposed to deteriorate but rather improve with the age of the tree.

On the shores of the Adriatic are many places celebrated for their wonderful figs. A curious tale is told of one, which, like the submerged forest of Chiassi, may be seen at clear tides beneath the sea. The fishermen say that if a man could dive and obtain a fig from this tree he would see a vision of the end of the world. The tree is supposed to have grown on rocky ground some distance from the coast, and during a volcanic eruption to have been submerged, and only discovered many years after by a belated fisherman on a clear summer night. He was rowing home over the pellucid waters of the Adriatic, tired after a long day's fishing, when he perceived a white seagull, or some miraculous white bird, continually diving over a certain spot in the sea not far distant from his boat. At length the bird, after many apparently futile attempts, came up to the surface of the water with something round in its beak, and the fisherman, overcome with curiosity, determined to

ascertain what this might be. He decoyed the
bird by throwing fish after fish into the sea on the
farther side of his boat, and as the bird, attracted
by the glistening scales of the fish, turned to dive
for them, it dropped the round object into the
water. The fisherman speedily possessed himself
of it, and on examining it discovered it to be a
fig of a remarkably large size, ripe and luscious.
He rowed to the spot where the bird had
been diving, and perceived beneath the water
a magnificent fig tree laden with fruit. Sea
anemones and star fish had made their homes in
its branches, and red and white coral adorned its
roots. He tasted the fig, and instantly fell into
a trance, in which state he was taken by an angel
and shown a miraculous vision, in which it was
revealed to him that at the end of the world the
souls of the blest would find themselves on an
island in the centre of the Adriatic, where they
would await a final consummation of events.
The world appeared to him coated with an
awful covering of ice and snow. No trees,
plants, or life of any kind remained upon it.
The rivers were frozen, and even the sea no
longer washed its icy coasts; only on the glorious
island and in the Adriatic all was as usual. The
sun rose daily in the east, the sunset dyed the
heavens with brilliant colours, and the clear waters

washed its shores. The island was supported upon the branches of the submerged fig tree, and as the chill of the frozen world sent an occasional icy blast over its waving foliage, he perceived that it slowly rose from the waters and was received into Paradise with all its inhabitants.

The fisherman, overcome with amazement, recovered from his swoon to find his boat still rocking upon the clear waves of the Adriatic, a brilliant moon overhead, and the night far advanced. Delighted at discovering the world still as he had left it, and the warm Southern breeze fanning his cheeks, he rowed home, and afterwards spent many weeks trying to discover the wonderful island of his vision. Neither it nor the fig tree has ever been seen since, but this story is a favourite tradition amongst the fishermen of the neighbourhood, and sometimes a fisher-lad will come home and excuse the paucity of his catch by saying, "I saw and followed the white bird, but discovered nothing, and have come home with neither fig nor fish."

THE PINE

"... From branch to branch
Along the piny forests on the shore
Of Chiassi, rolls the gathering melody
When Eolus hath from his cavern loosed
The southern winds ..."

"... Di ramo in ramo si raccoglie
Per la pineta in sul lito di Chiassi,
Quand Eolo Scirocco fuor discioglie."

Purg. xxviii. 19.

DANTE says that in the early morning, as he wandered in the wood which led to the Terrestrial Paradise, the little birds were all twittering to welcome dawn in the tops of the trees, and the rustling of the morning wind amongst the leaves "made a burden to their song." He compares the rustling of the wind to the wonderful sound—only to be realised by those who have heard it—of a heavy wind in a large forest extending over many miles of country, as he had himself heard it during his stay with

70

Guido da Polenta in the limitless pine woods of Chiassi.

The sound is extraordinary. An Eolian harp playing wild melodies mingled with the soft brooding tone of an under-harmony, gathering in intensity in the far distance of the inner forest, would make a wonderful "burden" to the happy wakening shrill twitter of the little feathered denizens of the woods; and the soul of the poet Dante would strangely respond to the depths of Nature's passion, underlying the simple joy of mere existence in her children.

The pine tree, with its stately height and resinous fragrance, shares with the fir many ancient traditions. A legend of Sicily records that the Saviour and His mother on their flight into Egypt were saved from Herod's soldiers by taking refuge in the shelter of a pine, which miraculously opened and formed walls around them until the danger was passed. The infant Saviour raised His hand to bless the tree, and from that time the form of a hand has always been apparent in the interior of the fruit, when cut straight through. For this reason the Sicilians hold the pine cone in great reverence.

Dante mentions a pine cone in the 31st canto of the *Inferno,* when he speaks of the large bronze pine "that tops St. Peter's Roman fane," which once ornamented the mole of Adrian, and being cast down by lightning, was placed on the belfry of St. Peter's Church.

A wreath of pine was a reward in the Isthmian games, and Ovid crowns his fauns with pine. This tree is dedicated in classical story to Cybele (or Rhea), the mother of the gods. Rhea loved Atys, a Phrygian shepherd, and gave to him the care of her temple in order that he might live in celibacy and serve her. Atys, unfortunately, fell in love with a nymph of the woods; and Rhea, infuriated with jealousy, changed him into a pine tree, under whose shade she sat and mourned, until Jupiter, to console her, decreed that the tree should always remain green.

Ovid says—

"'To Rhea grateful still the pine remains,
For Atys still some favour she retains.
He once in human shape her breast had warmed,
And now is cherished as a tree transformed!'"

THE PASSION FLOWER

"One tells how at Christ's suffering the wan moon
  Bent back her steps, and shadowed o'er the sun
  With intervenient disk, as she withdrew."

"Un dice, che la Luna si ritorse
  Nella passion di Cristo, e s'interpose,
  Per che'l lume del Sol giù non si porse."

Par. xxix. 97.

WHEN Dante uses the word "passion" in connection with Christ, he uses it to express our Lord's sufferings on the cross ; and in this way the word has been commonly employed in the title of the passion flower, which the legend tells us climbed the cross and spread its tendrils round the spots where the nails had been driven through the hands and feet of our Blessed Lord.

The passion flower is dedicated to St. Francis of Assisi, or rather to his bride, Dame Poverty. In many of our lonely country places it is always called the "poor flower." Indeed, this is its general name amongst the unlettered and fast-dying-out generation of those who keep alive the ancient legends by the unfailing traditions handed down from mouth to mouth amongst the people.

The countryman cuts its straggling sprays away from the sunny side of his cottage porch, and trains its delicate tendrils. He looks curiously at the flower, and sees the nails, the hammer, the soldier's lance, the five wound-prints, and the crown of thorns all clearly marked upon its face, and lifts the long tendrils that recall to him the ropes with which our Saviour was bound. But when his child asks him its name, he does not call it the "passion flower," but the "poor flower," and thus recalls, unconsciously, its later story, connected with St. Francis of Assisi and his bride Dame Poverty, and the little wood where St. Francis had so many of his marvellous visions, when rapt away in ecstatic communion with heaven.

In one of these visions St. Francis saw his bride, the Lady Poverty, standing beneath a luminous apparition of the cross, and as he beheld her she stretched her arms upwards, and gradually became transformed into the image of a passion flower, that grew up the stem and twined round the arms of the cross, covering each hole caused by the nails with a gleaming blossom.

THE PASSION FLOWER

St. Francis loved the passion flower, as he loved his bride, Dame Poverty, and after his death it was always associated with his name.

Dante, to whom all these ancient stories were familiar, speaks of the bride of St. Francis as

> " The dame . . . whom Francis did make his,
> Before the spiritual court, by nuptial bonds;"

and doubtless had not forgotten the legend of the passion flower when he adds—

> " With Christ she mounted to the cross,
> While Mary stood beneath."

> ". . . Dove Maria rimase giuso,
> Ella con Cristo salse in sulla croce."[1]

Dante stands in his visionary garden before the drooping passion flowers. The early morning dew yet lies upon them, and he dreams of Dame Poverty and the flowers that twined around the cross.

[1] *Par.* xi. 71.

THE OAK

" . . . Good beginnings last not
From the oak's birth, unto the acorn's setting."

" Che giù non basta buon cominciamento
Dal nascer della quercia al far la ghianda."
Par. xxii. 86.

DANTE employs the oak in an unusual sense, original and unconventional. He does not mention it as an emblem of strength or enduring power, but rather as he had gleaned impressions of it from his readings in the classics, where it is continually mentioned as the mother of mankind.

He is speaking of the weakness of human resolution, and it seems to occur to him as an additional reproach that born of so stalwart a parent as the oak, a man should not be able to make his good resolutions hold out from the oak's birth even to the bearing of its first acorn.

Virgil speaks of

" The nymphs and fauns and savage men who took
Their birth from trunks of trees and stubborn oak." [1]

And Juvenal in his sixth Satire, speaking of the beginning of the world, says that the human race were formed of clay, or born of the opening oak.

The ancients believed that as the oak was the progenitor of mankind, so, as a mother sustains her offspring from herself, the oak was bound to provide food and nourishment for the world. Ovid tells us that the simple food of the primal races consisted of acorns dropping from the tree of Jove, and Homer and Hesiod both say that the acorn was the common food of the Arcadians. In Italy and Southern Europe the primitive people dwelling in forests subsisted almost entirely upon the fruit of the oak, and Dante, looking upon it from the point of view of Italian tradition, uses it as a type of growing life, and a parable of time.

Beneath the spreading branches of the oak he seems to stand, and survey life from the point of view of the philosopher who would fain base his judgment upon the earliest beginnings of things. It is in Paradise where this simile of the oak occurs to him, where human nature is raised and

[1] *Æneid*, viii. 314-15.

glorified,—where, but a few lines farther on, he speaks of the Holy Triumph to which he hopes one day to return,—that he seems to remember with a pitying tenderness the early ignorant fables of the origin of human life, and to bewail the degeneration in the strength of human will, since the days when the early stalwart races of the world imagined that they took their origin from the mighty oaks of primeval forests.

LEGENDS

It is curious to note how the old Grecian belief in the sacred and supernatural character of the oak has lingered in Italy.

Professor de Gubernatus tells us that only about five-and-twenty years ago, a young peasant girl in the Campagna of Rome sought refuge beneath an oak during a terrific thunderstorm, and prayed to the Madonna to turn the lightning aside. A beautiful lady appeared in answer to her supplication, and stayed with her whilst the storm lasted, during which time no rain fell upon the oak, and the storm seemed to remove itself from their neighbourhood, though they could see it raging at a short distance round them. This miracle was reported to the curé of the district, who examined into it, and arranged that the shepherdess should be received into a convent, where, after an interval of preparation, she was eventually canonised.

A story of the same kind is told of a Tuscan shepherdess two centuries earlier, who was canonised under the name of Giovanna di Signa. In the district of Signa, near Genestra, her sacred oak is still shown by the villagers, who kneel and adore it. According to the legend, it sprang from Giovanna's crook, which she drove into the ground during a severe storm, calling all the shepherds and shepherdesses who were out with her to take shelter under it. A little chapel now stands on this spot, and the oak tree overshadowing it has the miraculous habit of throwing down everyone who attempts to climb it, though it will permit pious people to cut small twigs, which they carry home to their houses as a protection from the effects of storms, provided at the same time they call on the name of their patron saint or the Blessed Virgin.

We cannot credit Dante with a knowledge of these later traditions about the oak, but from the earliest times, when Virgil wrote of Jove's tree, whose roots descended to the infernal regions,[1]

---

[1] *Æneid*, Book iv.

tradition and legend have hovered around its hoary trunk. People have crept through to cure themselves of diseases, or pegged locks of their hair to "cross-oaks" to rid themselves of ague, or even fed their horses with oak buttons in order to change the colour of their coats, and superstition has played riot with these mighty trees from the days when the Dryads and Hamadryads made them their homes.

The oak has certainly a place in Dante's garden, and lends the shelter of its time-honoured traditions to the many graceful flowers of poesy and fancy growing around its mossy roots.

THE SYRINGA

" . . . Had I the skill
To pencil forth how closed the unpitying eyes
Slumbering, when Syrinx warbled (eyes that paid
So dearly for their watching) . . . "

" S'io potessi ritrar come assonnaro
  Gli occhi spietati, udendo di Siringa,
  Gli occhi, a cui più vegghiar costò sì caro."

Purg. xxxii. 64.

THE syringa flower is dedicated to the reed-nymph Syrinx, after whom, as a hollow-stemmed plant, it is named.

Syrinx fled from Pan to the river's edge, where she was changed into a reed, from which Pan made his pipes.

Sometimes at night, when the wind rustles through the slender reed-like branches of the syringa tree, one can fancy that a faint sound of music stirs the leaves. Pan, concealed amongst the scented white blossoms, is playing upon his

F   81

pipes, and awakening the echoes of the night with lamentations for his lost Syrinx.

The story of the Syrinx would well lend itself to song; and Dante mentions it, to express to his readers how his own senses became sweetly over-powered, and he sank into a slumber, as Argos did, when Mercury sang him to sleep with the legend of the Syrinx.

Argos, of the hundred eyes, had been given the beautiful nymph Io to watch and keep, and during his slumber she was stolen from him. So entrancing was Mercury's song about Syrinx that he forgot all his vigilance, and paid dearly for his neglect with the loss of his eyes, which Juno placed in the tail of her favourite peacock.

Dante alludes to this double story at the moment when, after his wondrous vision of the tree of knowledge, he falls into a deep slumber, overcome by light, colour, music, and the tense strain of interest. He says that if he had the skill to portray how Argos fell asleep listening to the story of the Syrinx, he could express, "like painter that with model paints," [1] the manner in which his own mind was slowly drawn from all present things, and sweet sleep absorbed the music in his soul.

[1] *Purg.* xxxii. 67.

APPLE-BLOSSOM

" The blossoming of that fair tree, whose fruit
  Is coveted by angels, and doth make
  Perpetual feast in heaven . . . "

        " . . . Li fioretti del melo,
          Che del suo pomo gli Angeli fa ghiotti
          E perpetue nozze fa nel cielo."

                                Purg. xxxii. 73.

IN this most beautiful canto of *Purgatorio*,
   Dante describes the blossoming of the
apple tree in the garden of the Earthly Paradise,
and the wondrous colour of the tender petals of
the apple-blossom against the sky.

The apple tree has always had a mystic significance,—in the classics its fruit is regarded as
an emblem of felicity, and the attaining of the
apple a symbol of bliss. Juno presents Jupiter
with golden apples which are kept in the gardens
of the Hesperides, and guarded by a dragon.
To Venus the apple is dedicated; there is the

fable of Atalanta and the golden apples which she stooped to pick up, and thus lost her race ; and the legend of the fatal apple cast by Discordia into the council of the gods, which, adjudged to Venus, caused the ruin of Troy.

The possession of the apple signifies bliss ; the desire and struggle for it cause infinite misfortune. And so in sacred lore whence these ancient fables take their origin, the apple—so desirable a fruit in itself—is the cause of the loss of Paradise.

In an earlier canto of *Purgatorio*, Dante speaks of that tree

> " . . . by which Christ was led
> To call on Eli, joyful when He paid
> Our ransom from His vein . . . "[1]

The tree which had caused our first parents to sin, and thus had brought a curse upon their descendants, which Christ expiated upon the cross.

St. Dorothea is always represented in old pictures with a basket of apples and roses in her hand, and this on account of the legend, which relates that, when she was on her way to execution, Theophilus, a lawyer, scoffed at her, saying, " When you reach Paradise, you may send me

[1] *Purg.* xxiii. 74.

some of the fruits and flowers which you say you will find there."

St. Dorothea replied, "I will do as you desire, O Theophilus." She immediately knelt down and prayed, and a beautiful boy appeared beside her, with a basket in his hand containing three magnificent roses, more exquisite than any ever seen on earth, and three large apples. Dorothea turned to him and said, "Take these to Theophilus, and tell him that I shall await him in the garden of Paradise, where these flowers and fruits were plucked."

She then bent her neck to the executioner, and the angel-boy went to Theophilus with the message and the present.

Theophilus was overcome with wonder and amazement. He tasted the apples, and touched the heavenly roses, and by the efficacy of the miracle, becoming converted to Christianity, he also obtained the crown of martyrdom, and thus followed St. Dorothea to the celestial gardens.

Dante's description of the apple tree in the garden of Paradise leads us once more to his boyhood, and his early acquaintance with the child Beatrice. There is a savour of this simplicity of childhood in the words he utters, when, awakened from his trance, and looking around for the star that had guided him so far, he exclaims, "Where is Beatrice?"

She is pointed out to him seated on the root of the apple tree, "beneath the fresh leaf,"[1] with the "associate choir" of angels surrounding her, and the air full of melody and song.

Surely with the melody of the birds above her and the song of spring in his heart, he had so seen her in the garden of his innocence and childhood, while the fresh apple-blossom fell and rested upon her hair!

[1] *Purg.* xxxii. 86.

THE MYRTLE

"A myrtle garland to enwreathe my brow."

"Le tempie ornar di mirto."
Purg. xxi. 90.

THE myrtle derives its name from Myrtilus,
the son of Mercury, who was changed into
a myrtle bush for treachery to his master.

Myrtilus served Oenomaus as chariot-driver.
Oenomaus, proud of his own skill, made known
that he would give his beautiful daughter, Hippodamia, to any suitor who could win a chariot-
race against himself.

The treacherous Myrtilus, bribed by Pelops,
who had entered for the competition, withdrew
the pin from his master's chariot-wheel. Oenomaus was killed, and Pelops obtained the hand
of the fair Hippodamia; but to avenge this act
of perfidy he threw Myrtilus into the sea. The
waves refused to receive the body of the traitor,

and cast it upon the shore, where it was changed into a bush, that ever after bore the name of the perfidious Myrtilus.

The temple of Venus at Rome was surrounded by a myrtle grove, and the Greeks adored Venus under the title of Myrtila, who, when she arose from the waves, was presented by the Hours with a scarf of many colours and a wreath of myrtle.

The myrtle tree is considered the emblem of immortality, but the ancients are said to have regarded its berries as a type of perfidy. When other trees have lost their foliage in the frosts of winter, the myrtle remains green, to remind us that life may yet lie hidden in the lap of death.

It adorns the brow of the poet, as a type of immortal fame, and has been employed by some writers as an emblem of Love, since where it grows it excludes all other plants.

The name of Poet,

"That name most lasting and most honour'd,"

"Quel nome che più dura, e più onora,"[1]

was Dante's own. Yet he only mentions the myrtle once in his *Divina Commedia*, and then it is to say that the brow of the poet Statius should have been adorned with it, in that charming

[1] *Purg.* xxi. 85.

scene where, betrayed by the lightning of a smile, Virgil makes himself known to his fellow-poet, and Statius attempts to embrace him, forgetting that they are both but unsubstantial shades.

Dante's thoughts do not often turn to the mythological fables of the myrtle tree. The love he bears to Beatrice—strong, tender, and bitter—is not a passion to play with. It drives him from the myths of heathen tradition to the reality of his deepest religious convictions. We never find him comparing his love for Beatrice to any affection inspired by a thought of Venus' myrtle grove, but rather to the Blessed Virgin and the rose of Paradise.

More probable is it that, when he paused before his myrtle tree, his thoughts may have recurred to the legend of St. Dominic, to whom he so often alludes in the course of his poem, and about whom there is a charming little story connected with the myrtle.

When St. Dominic was a child, his nurse gave him a myrtle bush, which he kept in an earthen vase on the floor of his chamber, and treasured highly.

Dante tells us that often in the watches of the night his nurse would come and find the little Dominic out of bed, and kneeling at his devotions when all the household slept.

One night, when thus engaged in prayer, the thought came to him that he must offer up his treasured plant, and obey the words of his Lord, who said, "Sell that thou hast, and give to the poor."

The following morning Dominic took his little plant out into the streets, and offered it to many passers-by. But they all smiled at the child, and rejected his sacrifice. At length a lady, clad in a dark-green robe, stopped him, and asked the price of the flower.

"I will sell it for a warm, thick cloak and two pairs of shoes," said the little Dominic. "Otherwise I cannot part from it."

"But what do you want with these?" said the lady, and added, "Come with me, and I will show you where we will take it."

They passed through many streets, and at length arrived at the door of a house, where they knocked, and a feeble voice inside bid them enter. By the window, on a little couch, lay a sick child, alone, and pale with suffering. Her eyes were bright and beautiful, and were fixed upon a dead flower in a broken vase by her bedside. She turned them as her visitors entered, and Dominic saw for the first time the light of approaching heaven in the eyes of a child—the look of one who is about to leave the earth, and to whom earthly things have become of small moment.

He approached the little bed, and, bending over her, showed her the plant.

" I have brought you a flower," he said, smiling, to her.

The child looked at the plant, and then at St. Dominic. A faint flush came into her cheeks, but she said nothing.

" It is the plant of Immortality," he continued, "and when you look at it you will remember that you can never die. When you grow too tired to see it clearly, the angels will come and carry you up to heaven in your sleep, where many myrtles bloom, and other flowers."

St. Dominic kissed the child, and went out with the lady into the street. She conducted him back the way they had come ; but no sooner had they arrived at the streets and squares known to him, than he suddenly found himself alone— his strange guide had disappeared, and he went on his way musing deeply.

That night the little Dominic lay awake, and prayed till dawn.

THE FIR

"... And as a fir
Upward from bough to bough less ample spreads."

"E come abete in alto si digrada
Di ramo in ramo ..."

Purg. xxii. 133.

THE fir tree is the king of the forest, as the birch is considered the queen. Dante compares a tree he sees during his journey in Purgatory, which was stately and "pleasant to the smell," to a fir tree, and describes a stream flowing near it to have been of "liquid crystal"— thus carrying on his simile by conveying the mind of the reader to the dry rocky soil and clean sand of the high places where firs abound. In this vision he has just been listening to the conversation of the two poets whom he most admired, Virgil and Statius, whose speech conveyed to his thoughts "mysterious lessons of sweet poesy," and here his poetry rises to a high pitch of grace and eloquence in the little sermon on self-denial given forth by the stately tree whose form and fragrance reminded him of the fir.

Professor de Gubernatus tells a story of a fir tree which stood by itself at Tarssok in Russia, and was much revered by the country people. Many trees growing solitary have been the objects of a regard almost like heathen worship amongst the superstitious and uneducated, and this fir tree, which had withstood storm and lightning for several hundred years, had become an object of great reverence to the Russian peasants living near it. At length, in a gale of wind, it fell, and great was the lamentation of the neighbourhood. The owner of the soil refused to make any profit from its trunk, which was eventually sold, and the money given to the Church.

Gerade writes of firs growing in Cheshire "since Noah's flood," which were at that time "overturned," and the people now find them beneath the soil, and in marshy places, and use them for fir-wood or fire-wood.

The resinous fir, like the pine, with its fragrant smell and stately form, was dear to the soul of the poet, and Dante alludes to it with the tender touch of a graceful and appreciative fancy.

THE NARCISSUS

THE narcissus is dedicated to the vain youth, beloved by Echo, who gazed at his own image in the fountain, and was changed into the flower that bears his name—ever after to bend over the mirror in self-contemplation. The cup in the centre of the flower contains the "tears of Narcissus," as Virgil remarks, when speaking of the bees who gather their honey from these early spring blossoms—

"Some placing within the house the tears of Narcissus."[1]

There is something curiously both repellent and attractive about this flower. Its perfume is

---

[1] *Georgic*, iv.

powerful and narcotic, but after the first short ecstasy of pleasure it soon palls upon the senses.

The narcissus is supposed to have been the flower employed by Pluto to entice Proserpine down into the infernal regions—

> ". . . In that season, when her child
> The Mother lost; and she, the bloomy Spring."

> ". . . Nel tempo che perdette
> La madre lei, ed ella primavera."[1]

And Sophocles alludes to it as the garland of Proserpine.

In the North no bride may wear it in her wedding wreath, lest she bring ill-luck upon the first year of her married life.

Yet the narcissus appears at a first glance one of the most exquisite of flowers. It rises from the earth in the early summer, and the purity of its delicate white petals contrasting with the deep red slender ring in the centre, its wonderful perfume, and the grace with which its head is poised upon a slender stem, all combine to produce a sensation of wonder and admiration.

Surely it might dispute the palm even with the lily. Yet it has seldom been able to excite in the breast of any poets sentiments other than those of a purely earthly affection. Its name never

[1] *Purg.* xxviii. 50.

occurs at all in sacred allegory; and Dante, who
has an unfailing perception in such matters, first
alludes to it in his *Inferno*, where he makes the
wretched soul of an impostor, who is railing upon
a companion in misfortune, exclaim—

> " . . . No urging wouldst thou need
> To make thee lap Narcissus' mirror up!"[1]

And in the *Paradiso*, where he again quotes the
fable, he only uses it as a contrast, saying that he
is seized with a "delusion opposite to that which
raised between the man and fountain amorous
flame!"[2]   For in the heaven of the moon where
he has arrived, the images he sees are real, not
imaginary, though he fell into the error of mis-
taking them at first for reflected semblances.
These images so faintly seen by Dante are the
souls of those who had been compelled on earth
to violate religious vows, and Beatrice says of
them, "Now no longer will their feet stray from
the desires of purity they had conceived upon
earth."

In the legend of Proserpine, who was enticed
by Pluto into the Inferno, we are told that the
ravishing perfume of the narcissus so stupefied
Ceres' senses that she did not perceive her
daughter's danger; and the narcotic so dulled

---

[1] *Inf.* xxx. 128.   [2] *Par.* iii. 18.

the senses of the lovely nymph herself, that, laden with armfuls of the fateful flower, she presented herself at the very gates of Dis.

In Sir Frederic Leighton's picture, where Proserpine is rescued again from the depths of the earth, Ceres—as Mother Earth—stands above, with outstretched arms, to welcome her ; and Proserpine is represented as coming up like a spring flower, with the pale tints of the mauve crocus, the dainty primrose, and the white narcissus in her floating robes.

Dante knew well that the narcissus belongs of right to the earth, the rose and lily to Paradise.

THE BRIAR-ROSE

" Nel giallo della rosa sempiterna."

Par. xxx. 124.

I N Dante's garden are roses of every colour,
red, white, and yellow, and the red briar
(Southern sister to the wild-rose of our English
country hedges) deserves a special mention, as
Dante is the only poet who has ever accurately
described its wonderfully brilliant gold and flame
colour.

When Beatrice first appears to him, after his
ascent into Purgatory, he describes her as—

" Vestita di color di fiamma viva,"[1]

clad in a robe the colour of living flame! Can
anyone read this line who has ever seen the
blossom of the Southern briar-rose—with its pale
gold beneath the petals, and wondrous flame

[1] *Purg.* xxx. 33.

colour above—without a vivid picture of the flower arising at once in his mind's eye?

I have always imagined that Beatrice appears to Dante in this vision clad in one continuous petal of this beautiful flower. The scene is laid in the open air, under a roseate sky. Angelic hands are scattering flowers around her. Dante—who here draws his similes from Nature—is not thinking of a devouring fire in the colour in which he arrays her: that would be alien to the whole picture. He is thinking of a flame-coloured flower sheltered in green foliage ("sotto verde manto"), such as he may often have seen in the garden of his fancy.

Certainly colours have their mystic significance for him,—red for Love, and green for Hope,—but in this vision the flowers are more to him than their colours. He clothes Beatrice in the very flower that to him represents the Blessed Virgin, as he imagines her to be clothed in Divine Love.

The Southern briar-rose should at least have a place in his garden, if for no other reason than that Dante has clad his Beatrice, and Nature her queen of flowers, for one occasion and in one variety, with the self-same colour of living flame.

THE PALM

" For that he beareth palm
Down unto Mary, when the Son of God
Vouchsafed to clothe Him in terrestrial weeds. "

" Egli è quegli, che portò la palma
Giù a Maria, quando'l Figliuol di Dio
Carcar si volle della nostra salma."
Par. xxxii. 112.

" For the cause
That one brings home his staff
Enwreathed with palm."

" . . . Per quello
Che si reca il bordon di palma cinto."
Purg. xxxiii. 77.

SACRED writers, when wishing to describe what is beautiful and full of dignity and service, have continually employed the palm as a typical emblem of majesty and rectitude. King David's promise to the just is that he shall grow up and flourish as a young palm tree; and as with the Jews, so in the Christian Church, it was always a symbol of triumph. At the feast of tabernacles branches of palm were carried in the synagogues, and the children waved it on Christ's triumphal entrance into Jerusalem.

So whenever Dante employs the palm it is as an emblem of joy and grace. The Angel Gabriel "beareth palm down to Mary," and the pilgrim returns home in triumph from the Holy Land with his staff enwreathed with palm.

The branches of palm brought home by pilgrims from Palestine were highly treasured by their possessors, and were supposed to be safeguards against robbers, diseases, the evil eye, and all the many ills flesh was more specially heir to in the turbulent Middle Ages.

A palmer from Palestine, on his way back to Italy, spent the night with other pilgrims at a small hostel in the plains, beneath the glorious Alps, which he had just, at imminent risk of life, surmounted with his companions.

He was worn to a shadow, his garb tattered and travel-stained, but the light of triumph and achievement illumined his countenance.

On awakening in the morning after their first night in the fruitful plains of their native land, a report reached the pilgrim troupe that fever, in a specially virulent form, had broken out in an adjoining village. The pilgrims hurriedly broke up their camp and started southwards, to reach their homes by different routes; but the aged palmer inquired of their informant if there was any priest to give aid and consolation to the dying in the distressed village, or any Christian man to nurse and attend on them.

On hearing that two friars of the order of St. Francis, who had come to their assistance, had themselves succumbed to the disease, the palmer took his staff and hurried instantly to the scene of action. Here he diligently nursed the infected cases; but in every instance, on entering a house, his first action was to wave his treasured palm branch over the heads of all the inmates not yet infected with the disease, who in no instance, after this ceremony, were attacked by it.

The sick kissed it and were speedily healed, and on the cessation of the fever in the village a public thanksgiving was offered to God for the benefits wrought through His faithful pilgrim servant, by the branch of the sacred palm brought with so many hardships and sufferings from the Holy Land.

This legend is only one out of many with which Dante may have been acquainted, and which may have helped to clothe the palm in his mind with all the joyous attributes he associates with it. In another story of the twelfth century, brigands are supposed to have fallen prostrate around a band of noble pilgrims they had attacked, at the sight of the holy branches from the East, and on kissing the palms with reverence, this further act of grace induced them to give up their lawless lives and return to peaceable citizenship.

Beatrice in speaking to Dante, when she is conducting him through the latter part of Purgatory towards Paradise, tells him that since his understanding is still hardened by contact with the world, and he is too dazzled by the mysteries she is revealing to him to understand them fully as yet, he must try and carry back with him to earth the imprint of her words upon his mind, to prove where he has been, as the pilgrim carries home the sacred trophy of the palm enwreathed around his staff.

THE VINE

" E'en thou went'st forth in poverty and hunger
   To set the goodly plant, that from the Vine
   It once was, now is grown unsightly bramble."

" Chè tu entrasti povero e digiuno
   In campo a seminar la buona pianta,
   Che fu già vite, ed ora è fatta pruno."

                            Par. xxiv. 109.

IN the lines quoted above, Dante speaks to St. Peter, whom he encounters in Paradise, about that " goodly plant " the Church, which was started in poverty and hunger, and " from the Vine it once was," had become so full of corruptions. St. Peter is examining him on the subject of faith, and Dante, well versed in the tenets of the Church, seems to pass through this trying ordeal with satisfaction.

The vine that grows in his garden is a wondrous and mystic plant. It is the very incarnation of the Christian faith, the emblem of Christ Himself, and the boughs and leaves and tendrils are the grafted body of the faithful.

Dante says that St. Dominic

> " . . . did set himself
> To go about the vineyard . . . "[1]

that is, to work in Christ's garden, and the vine is continually used by him as a type of the Christian Church.

For legend or story connected with it we must refer to biblical lore. In the New Testament it is more frequently mentioned than any other plant, and it is from thence that Dante would have drawn most of his ideas and similes. In Italy the people have a superstitious reverence for a vine, and consider that in its shelter no harm or danger can affect them. A little child has been seen to run and hold up its arms to the shelter of a drooping vine when pursued by a companion, and in playful fear. The pursuer might not follow with harmful intent to the shelter of the vine, though when outside again the romp was renewed. The peasant mother standing by remarked that this was " a sacred tree," and made the sign of the cross when alluding to it. In Lombardy the peasants make small crosses of the wood of the vine, and hold

[1] *Par.* xii. 86.

them in special reverence.   The bacchanalian rites of old, with wild ceremonies and mad intoxication, have given place to Christian teaching, and even the vine has become the symbol of self-restraint, and is made into an emblem of suffering and renunciation, as the will rolls onward towards better things, " by love impelled."

THE
STAR OF BETHLEHEM

" And Truth was manifested as a star in heaven."

" E come stella in cielo, il ver si vide."

Par. xxviii. 87.

THE star of Bethlehem—beloved and treasured flower in thousands of our cottage
gardens—is well known by all the country-folk to
be the lineal descendant of that star which once
appeared in the East, to proclaim in the birth
of the Saviour the greatest Truth that earth has
ever known.

The mysterious appearance and disappearance
of this star has given rise to poetical legends
without end.

Some say that it fled away like a meteor into
space, to reappear at the second coming of Christ ;

and some, that it sank to the earth and burst
into constellations of myriads of white starry
flowers around the stable door where the infant
Saviour lay. It is horological, and never unfolds
its petals before eleven o'clock in the morning,
and is very abundant in the neighbourhood of
Samaria.

Each blossom is encircled with leaves of a
dazzling whiteness, and the flower has always
borne the name of the " Star of Bethlehem."

" In the morning," saith the legend, " Joseph,
the foster-father of the fair Babe, went forth
in the yet flickering dawn to meditate upon
his wondrous visions of the night. At his feet
—as if planted by angel hands—the starry
splendour of a hundred white blossoms blazed
forth.

" The star, also, had come to earth, unable
to remain in the spangled glory of the sky,
when its Creator lay humbled as a human babe
beneath.

" St. Joseph gathered the flowers and brought
them in to the Blessed Virgin. ' Behold,' he
said, ' the Star from the East hath fallen and
multiplied before Him ! ' "

Reared from his boyhood in the devout and
poetical imagery of ancient Church tradition,
stories such as these must often have passed

through the mind of Dante when he walked in the fair garden of his childhood, before his feet had strayed into the dark forest of maturer life.

No poet has ever loved the stars more than Dante—the stars for which Beatrice so soon forsook this lower life.

Each of the three great divisions of his *Divina Commedia* ends with a reference to the stars. The last word of the *Inferno, Purgatorio,* and *Paradiso* is "stelle."

He speaks of the "morning star,"[1] of the stars, those "glorious and thick-studded gems"[2] that like costly jewels inlay the sky, and of Truth that was "manifested as a star in heaven."[3]

When he has reached the empyrean, and sees the souls of the blest adoring in the actual presence of God, he exclaims—

> " . . . O trinal beam
> Of individual Star, that charm'st them thus,
> Vouchsafe one glance to gild our storm below!"

> " O, trina luce! Che in unica Stella
> Scintillando a lor vista sì gli appaga,
> Guarda quaggiù, alla nostra procella!"[4]

---

[1] *Par.* xxxii. 108.   [2] *Par.* xviii. 115.
[3] *Par.* xxviii. 87.   [4] *Par.* xxxi. 28.

THE STAR OF BETHLEHEM

The birth of the Saviour is also a subject upon which Dante loves to linger. He says—

> " We stood, immovably suspended ; like to those,
> The shepherds, who first heard in Bethlehem's field
> That song ; till ceased the trembling, and the song
> Was ended . . . "

> " Noi stavamo immobili e sospesi,
> Come i pastor che prima udîr quel canto,
> Fin che il tremar cessò, ed ei compièsi." [1]

---

[1] *Purg.* xx. 139.